S

J

This book belongs to:

• • • • • • • • • • • • • •

SIMON SPOTLIGHT
An imprint of Simon & Schuster Children's Publishing Division
1230 Avenue of the Americas
New York, New York 10020

Designed and produced by Les Livres du Dragon D'Or

Manufactured in Italy

First Edition   10 9 8 7 6 5 4 3 2 1

ISBN 0-689-81632-4

Balloons
and
Other Fun Things

Gravity
Seeds and
How They Grow
Balloons
In the Pool

Simon Spotlight

GRAVITY

There is an invisible force within the Earth which is called gravity. Gravity keeps everything from flying away. That is why we stay on the ground!

Ouch!
"Why don't those apples stay up in the tree?" Huckle asks. "It's because of gravity," Lowly replies.

f you knock something over and it falls on the ground, it's the Earth's
gravity that is pulling it down.

Gravity keeps everything in its place.

Without it, everything would float around in the air!

Just imagine! Everyone and everything would fly away if it weren't for gravity!

Sergeant Murphy would have a hard time directing traffic, and Bananas Gorilla wouldn't be able to hold on to his bananas! Even Hilda would be as light as a feather!

When it rains, it's gravity, too, that pulls the raindrops down from the clouds. We can be thankful for gravity!

"Look at all the apples I've picked up for you," Huckle tells Lowly. "Thank you, Huckle! And thanks to gravity, too!" says Lowly.

SEEDS AND HOW THEY GROW

Did you know that plants—from great big trees to tasty fruits—all come from seeds? Now, where do the seeds come from? Let's find out!

Bon appetit, Huckle and Lowly! "Another one!" exclaims Lowly, spitting a watermelon seed onto his plate.

"Am I happy that corn doesn't have seeds!" Huckle says. "Sure, it does," Lowly replies. "You are eating them right now Each kernel of corn is a seed."

You can find seeds in every vegetable and fruit. Some seeds are hidden, such as appleseeds. Other seeds show on the outside, like those on strawberries.

But seeds need your help to grow! Dig some holes in the ground, drop in the seeds, and cover them again with earth. Then sprinkle water each day on the seeds you have planted and watch what grows!

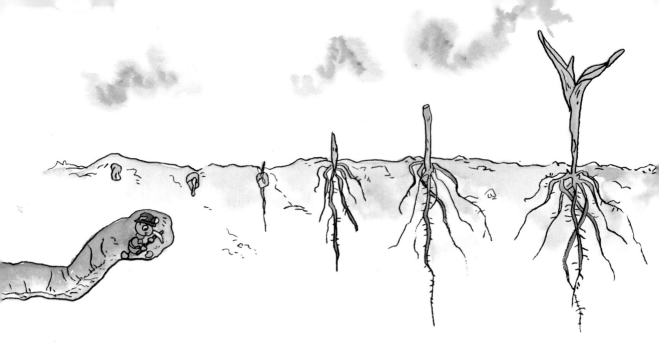

As the seeds grow, they spread roots into the soil below. The seeds begin to sprout leaves and stems above ground. With water and sunshine, the seeds will keep growing into plants.

You can also find seeds in flowers and weeds. If you blow the seeds off
a dandelion, you may soon see new dandelions growing where their
seeds have fallen.

Each tree was just a seed before it grew. Isn't that amazing?
Watch out for that falling pinecone! It is full of pine seeds waiting to become big pine trees some day!

"I never knew seeds could taste so good!" Huckle exclaims. *Mmmm!*

BALLOONS

There are all sorts of balloons.
Some go high up in the air.
Some stay down on the ground.
Do you know why?

"Why is it that Bruno's balloons float and mine doesn't?"
Huckle wonders.
"Because Bruno's balloons are filled with helium," Lowly says.
"It is a gas that is lighter than air and makes balloons float."

"Let's play with Bruno's balloons, Lowly!" Huckle says.

Uh-oh! Watch out, Lowly! The balloon is carrying you up!

Luckily, Rudolph von Flugel is nearby with his hot-air balloon! "Rudolph, please help me rescue Lowly!" Huckle yells.

"Anchors aweigh!"
Rudolph von Flugel shouts.
He turns on a special burning
flame which heats the air
inside the giant balloon.

Hot air is lighter than
cool air, and so Rudolph's
balloon rises high into
the sky!

Hurry, Rudolph!
Hurry, Huckle!

Now, a helium balloon can't go up forever. High in the sky, Lowly's balloon finally bursts. *Pop!* Uh-oh, Lowly!

Fortunately, Rudolph and Huckle are there just in time to catch their friend!

Ooof!
"That was close!" says Lowly.
"Thank you, Huckle and Rudolph!"

"Enough adventures for today," Rudolph von Flugel says. "Let's go back down to Busytown!"

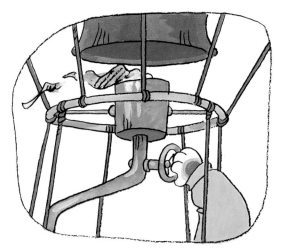

He turns off the burner to cool the air in the balloon and down they go, gently to the ground.

"Gee," says Lowly. "Balloons are fun when they go up, but they're even better when they come down!"

IN THE POOL

Going to the pool is lots of fun! But before you jump in, always remember: Swim only when a lifeguard is on duty. Here are some more rules you need to know!

The sun is out and the sky is blue. What a perfect day for going in the pool! You can jump, dive, splash, and float, but first of all, you must learn a couple of swimming pool rules!

Mr. Frumble climbs up the ladder to the diving board to prepare to dive.

Tweet! Tweet!
"Watch out, Mr. Frumble!" the lifeguard warns. "Bruno is right underneath you. You must call out to him and wait until he moves."

Before you dive, don't forget to *always* look below first!

Be careful, Sally! *Never* run around the pool deck.
When the deck is wet, it is very slippery.

Whoa! See what I mean?   Thank you, Lowly!

These are just a couple of rules to remember to make swimming at the pool not only fun, but safe, too!

Have fun, everyone!
Splish-splash!

1. Huckle's House
2. Hilda's House
3. Sgt. Murphy's
4. Pig Family House
5. Mr Frumble's
6. Fire Station
7. Town Hall
8. Mr Fixit's House
9. Busytown Hospital
10. Schoolhouse
11. Mr Gronkle's
12. Sprout's Farm

Busytown Airport

The Recycling Plant

April Rhino's House

Stadium

The Port